BEST
GIRL

BEST GIRL

SYLVIA MAULTASH WARSH

RAVEN BOOKS
an imprint of
ORCA BOOK PUBLISHERS

Library and Archives Canada Cataloguing in Publication

Warsh, Sylvia Maultash
Best girl / Sylvia Maultash Warsh.
(Rapid reads)

Issued also in electronic formats.
ISBN 978-1-55469-897-4

I. Title. II. Series: Rapid reads
PS8595.A7855B47 2012   C813'.6   C2011-907539-3

First published in the United States, 2012
Library of Congress Control Number: 2011942469

Summary: A young aspiring musician's life is turned upside down when
she begins to learn the truth about her long-dead parents. (RL 2.6)

MIX
Paper from
responsible sources
FSC® C016245

*Orca Book Publishers is dedicated to preserving the environment and has
printed this book on paper certified by the Forest Stewardship Council®.*

Orca Book Publishers gratefully acknowledges the support for
its publishing programs provided by the following agencies:
the Government of Canada through the Canada Book Fund and the
Canada Council for the Arts, and the Province of British Columbia
through the BC Arts Council and the Book Publishing Tax Credit.

Design by Teresa Bubela
Cover photography by Getty Images

ORCA BOOK PUBLISHERS
PO Box 5626, Stn. B
Victoria, BC Canada
V8R 6S4

ORCA BOOK PUBLISHERS
PO Box 468
Custer, WA USA
98240-0468

www.orcabook.com
Printed and bound in Canada.

15 14 13 12 • 4 3 2 1

For Jerry, as always.
And for my muses, Nathaniel and Jessica.

CHAPTER ONE

My life changed on October 23, 2010. Suddenly I didn't know who I was. Before the phone call, here's what I knew: I was adopted. My real parents died in a car crash when I was four. Shelley was the only mother I've ever known. As soon as I could understand, she told me I was adopted. Shelley's husband—I never thought of him as my father—wasn't home much. When he lost his job, he went out west to work in the oil fields.

I didn't have a lot of friends. It was mostly Shelley and me. I always cared too much and didn't want to get hurt. Because people let you down. People are liars.

All the time I was growing up, Shelley and I argued. She never saw things my way. Then she could stay mad for days and not speak to me. In the end she'd be all lovey-dovey, as if nothing had happened. When I was a kid, I was always relieved when she started talking again. It was hard living with someone who ignored you. Once I was a teenager, though, I didn't mind being left alone. When she saw it didn't bug me, she gave up the silent treatment.

The best thing she ever did for me was make me take piano lessons. She said her own family was too poor to pay for lessons when she was a kid. Her mother laughed when she asked for them and said she was too stupid to play piano.

Shelley loved listening to music (mostly bad music). She couldn't hold a tune. To her, musicians walked on water.

Where she got the money for the piano I never knew. It's been there since I can remember. When I was young, I hated practicing. I was always a little rebel. Anything Shelley wanted, I didn't. So she made me feel guilty. Her usual line—if she could scrounge together the money for lessons, the least I could do was practice. She found a music student a few blocks away who charged less than the going rate, but it was still a lot of money for a hairdresser. She said she had to cut and style two heads of hair to pay for one hour of lessons. Sometimes we ate Kraft Dinner to make up for it.

So I pouted while practicing my scales, up and down, up and down the keys. Until I realized I was good at it. Then I just *pretended* to hate it. Shelley didn't understand why the piano teacher started me on Mozart and Bach. "Doesn't the teacher know any Billy Joel or Phil Collins?" she'd ask. I'd roll my eyes and say, "She's teaching me music that doesn't suck." I stopped piano lessons when I was fifteen because I got interested in the guitar. My voice wasn't bad either. But I only sang when Shelley wasn't home.

The radio in her hair salon was stuck on the "easy listening" channel, so those old songs were background music while I was growing up. They made me want to hurl. Even going into *Shelley's*, the salon she owned on the Danforth, made me want to hurl. It was old and dingy and badly needed a facelift. Her customers were old too. When I was younger, some of them would comment on how I didn't look anything like Shelley. I took that as an insult because Shelley was hot. Tall and thin with a long neck. Her ears were perfect little shells with earlobes. I was always jealous of her ears because mine were ugly. They were big and flat with thin round edges like clamshells. And no earlobes! She laughed when I complained, and said no one would notice my ears if I wore my hair long.

I thought Shelley would be happy when I told her I wanted to sing with a band. But she wasn't. It seemed to make her nervous. And I didn't even tell her I would be playing guitar, not piano, for accompaniment. She said I needed to make a living, so she taught me to cut hair. I fought at first, but then I started to like it. I had complete control over someone for an hour. They sat in my chair and they couldn't move. Not if they wanted a really cool haircut. Shelley showed me how to dye hair, and after that I was the only one she trusted to do hers. She liked to change her hair color with the season. I dyed it a streaky blond for the summer.

Then I pulled the rug out from under her feet. Without telling her, I registered for an apprentice job at a salon in Yorkville where the customers had style. I had to take classes in a hair school for a couple of hours a week too. The boss liked me and printed out some business cards with my name.

Shelley was mad, but impressed with the cards and the snazzy address.

I hadn't told her ahead of time because I knew it would be a hassle. She'd yell and call me ungrateful. Maybe I was. But I wanted more than *Shelley's* salon. She was really mad when I moved out—but hey, I was twenty-three! Now that I was making my own money, I could afford a studio apartment near the subway. I was *so* out of there. Couldn't live with her anymore—she was a control freak. Okay, so we both had control issues. Even so, last month I came to her shop on a Sunday to dye her hair mauve-red for the fall (her choice). She was almost fifty but looked good for her age.

*   *   *

But back to the phone call. A woman named Diane called, asking for Amanda Jane Moss. That was me.

"You don't know me," she said. "I was a friend of your mother's. She was a good person."

"How do you know Shelley?"

"I mean your real mother."

"What?"

"She asked me to give you something. Can I come by this afternoon?"

"There's some mistake. My mother died twenty years ago."

"Is your birthday December third, nineteen eighty-six?"

"How d'you know?"

"Your mother told me. Her name was Carol Allan. You were born Amanda Allan. You were adopted by Shelley and Stephen Moss. Carol...your mother and I worked together. We were friends."

I was speechless. This was the first time I'd heard my birth mother's name. Shelley always said the agency wouldn't tell her who my parents were, only that they had died in a crash.

Then she said, "I'm sorry to have to tell you—Carol died last week. It was cancer. I'm so sorry." There was a pause. "Please tell Shelley."

In a daze, I gave her my address. Why did my mother give me away? She was alive all this time! It was like a knife in my chest. I could've met her.

It was Monday, so I had the day off. I stewed for half an hour, getting madder and madder. Then I called Shelley.

"You liar!"

"What're you talking about?"

"You lied to me! About my mother."

I felt the shock over the phone. I knew her too well. After my father left for the last time, there were just the two of us.

"Who told you that?"

"Nobody you know."

"You talked to someone…"

"She was alive all these years and you didn't want me to meet her."

"No, no, that's not true. You don't understand…I…I was trying to protect you."

"Why did you lie to me?"

"There are some things…better not to know."

That was just like her. "I'll never meet her now."

"What're you talking about?"

"She's dead."

A long pause. "It's better that way."

"That's a horrible thing to say."

"Believe me…"

"I'll never forgive you."

I heard a sharp intake of breath. Good.

"I didn't tell you because—she was evil."

I slammed down the phone.

*　*　*

Diane showed up at my door, a worn-out woman around forty who must have been pretty once. She wore a rain jacket over her jeans and carried a black canvas tote bag in one hand, her purse in the other. Nice hair—kind of a pageboy dyed chestnut. She stared at me as if she'd seen a ghost.

"Wow, you look just like your mother. When she was young, I mean."

I asked her in, nervous and excited both. When she took off her jacket, she was wearing a green scrub tunic. We sat down on my old IKEA sofa, her purse and tote bag between us.

"Are you a nurse?" I asked.

Diane smiled and nodded. She said no more about herself, and I didn't ask.

I went on to what I really wanted to know. "What was she like?"

Diane looked away, remembering. "She was strong. Inside, you know? She knew who she was. No bullshit. Pretty though."

She turned to me. "Dark hair and white skin. Blue eyes. Like you."

I got a shiver down my back.

"Here's some pictures." Diane took a manila envelope out of the tote bag and handed it to me.

I peered inside the envelope. My heart jumped. I pulled out a photo.

A cute young couple with lots of hair smiled at the camera in front of Niagara Falls. She wore a short white dress. He was in a suit. They looked happy.

"That's Carol and Freddy on their wedding day," she said. "They were both twenty-one."

Freddy. My father's name was Freddy!

I turned the photo over. Someone had written in: *September 20, 1985.* I was born one year later.

I took out more photos, staring at the mother I would never meet. It was like looking into my own face. The same wary eyes, the high forehead. Then I *was* looking into my own face. Me as a baby. Then as a toddler. My mother, a bit older, sitting on a stoop holding me on her knee, both of us smiling like crazy. There was something weirdly familiar about that stoop. Could I really remember it from when I was that young?

"That's your dad," said Diane.

I picked up a picture of Freddy. His longish hair was pulled back into a ponytail, his head turned a bit so I could see his ear. And there it was! The clamshell ear I hated on me. No earlobe. Only it looked good on him.

Tears filled my eyes. Embarrassed, I stuck my hand into the envelope again and pulled out something else. A faded flyer: three young guys playing music onstage. The Tranzac Club. The date at the bottom was August 2, 1984.

"That was Freddy's band," said Diane.

"My father was a musician?" Young and skinny, Freddy played the guitar, looking spaced out on bliss.

"Vandal Boss. They did okay."

"The one with Stu Van Dam?" I asked.

Vandal Boss was local, and I was interested in bands so I'd heard of them, though they never made the big time. Their claim to fame was Stu Van Dam. I peered more closely at the shot. The lead dude in the middle practically chewed on the microphone. That was Stu. He'd become a star on his own in the nineties with a hit song—they still played it on the radio. Blond. Full of himself. Behind them sat a guy on drums. I was trying to remember what happened to them. They'd dropped off the radar.

My father had played with a band! I was excited. That's where I got it from!

"Where's Freddy now?" I wanted to meet him!

Diane looked at me strangely. "You really don't know?"

"Know what?"

She hesitated. "I met your mother when I worked in the infirmary. She got sick a few years ago. The chemo helped for a while, but then...I got to know her. She was a kind person. She didn't do what they said."

CHAPTER TWO

"What do you mean?" I asked.

Diane squirmed on the sofa and looked away. "It's hard for me to tell you."

I got a bad feeling about what was coming.

"It was a prison infirmary."

"She was in jail?" I gasped in spite of myself. "What did she do?"

Diane cleared her throat. "She was in for murder."

"Murder?"

Diane stared straight ahead.

"Who?" But I knew before she said it.

"They said she killed Freddy. But she didn't do it."

My hand went to my mouth. Maybe Shelley was right. Maybe it was better not to know. I was the kid of a murderer. Tears dripped onto my arm.

Diane sat on the edge of the sofa, watching me. "This is what Carol told me: Vandal Boss toured around the country. Freddy was always out of town. Groupies followed them wherever they went. They liked Freddy. He was the quiet one. He could've had any of them, Carol said. She knew, but she was stuck at home with"— she looked at me—"a baby. They always argued when he came home, she said. One night Carol was asleep when he came back from some gig. She woke up when she heard screaming. She ran downstairs and found him lying inside the front door. A knife in his chest."

I was breathless. But I had to think. "She didn't see anybody?"

Diane shook her head. "Nobody saw anything. The cops said she planned it, so that made it first-degree murder. She got life."

She'd been alive all this time. My brain had to adjust to that idea. "But if she didn't do it…" I said. "Who did?"

Diane shrugged. "She was sure it was a jealous boyfriend. She warned Freddy— all his fooling around would catch up with him one day."

"She didn't see anybody outside the house?"

"Nothing."

"Did anyone check around to find the guy?"

"She didn't have any names. Freddy didn't talk about his girlfriends. The cops concentrated on her. They said it was almost always the jealous spouse."

I hated being negative, but they had a point.

She must've sensed my doubt. "Here." She lifted the tote bag and held it out to me. "Some of the women prisoners wrote to you. And there's a notebook. They found it under her mattress when they were cleaning out her cell."

I pulled out a lined notebook, the kind kids use in school. Diane watched as I opened it to the first page.

January 12, 1992

Hey, Universe, You happy now? Everything I had is gone—the only man I ever loved. My little girl. And my freedom. What about the guy who killed Freddy? I'll bet he's living in a nice house and driving a fancy car. I see red when I think of him out there. I try to picture what he looks like so I can hate him better, but all I can see is devil horns on his ugly head. I keep going over that last night in my head—me waking up in bed. The scream. Me coming downstairs. Freddy lying in the hall. The knife, the blood…No! I won't think about that. Who was it? Who took my Freddy from me?

I felt dazed. My head was going to explode. I couldn't move when Diane stood up.

"Here's my address and phone number if you want to reach me." She put a slip of paper down on my coffee table.

I couldn't get a word out, but somehow she understood and quietly left. I turned the page of the notebook.

January 19, 1992
Hey, Universe, All the women here say they're innocent and that they're in jail by mistake. I don't bother to say, Me too. I know no one will believe me. Every night I pray I'll wake up from the nightmare, and every morning I wake up in this cell.

January 26, 1992

Hey, Universe, I dreamt about Mandy again. I can't stand thinking I'm not there while she's growing up. She'll never know me. Or worse, she'll hear about me and think I killed her father. She's too young to understand now. And when she's old enough, she'll be in the middle of a new life. She'll have new parents that love her, and the best thing for her is if she never knows I exist. It hurts so much that I'll never see my little girl again.

I tried to remember being five. That's how old I was in 1992 when she wrote the note. My chest felt tight.

I flipped numbly through the pages in a daze. The letters to the Universe were all variations on the same themes. She missed Freddy. She missed me. She was innocent. She had written once a week for nearly two years. A hundred pages; that was all the notebook had. Her last entry:

November 19, 1994

Hey, Universe, No one will ever believe I'm innocent; I have to accept that. I'll never see little Mandy again, I have to accept that too. I have to move on. I'll never stop loving Freddy. The only thing I have left of him is his guitar. I keep seeing us when we were teenagers and he taught me the chords. I hold it close to me and I can almost smell him in the wood. The women here like to listen to me play. They say it calms them down. Christmas is coming, and they want me to give a little concert. Maybe a sing-along. They hum the songs when I practice. I'm trying to figure out the chords to some carols. Maybe after Christmas we can put together a choir! Wouldn't that be rich? I'd be teaching music again.

Another musician! I had genes on both sides.

Diane said they found the notebook under her mattress. That meant she didn't want anyone reading it. So when she said she was innocent, it was like she was talking to herself. Didn't that mean she was telling the truth?

I found at least twenty notes from the women in another manila envelope, some scrawled and childlike, some neat and carefully written.

Dear Mandy, The cops should burn in hell for putting your mom in here. She was no killer. Patty.

Dear Mandy, Your mom was the best. Rest in Peace. Lottie.

Dear Mandy, If it wasn't for your mom and the choir, I'd be dead. There was nothing to live for till I started to sing. I owe her. Dale.

Dear Mandy, Your mom shouldna been here. It was wrong cause she didn't kill no one. Her music helped me go on. Vi.

There was a business-sized envelope in the bag. The letterhead said it was from a lawyer named Randall Webb. I pulled out a single page.

Dear Carol,

I'm afraid I have bad news. Our appeal was turned down. In his explanation, the judge said there was no new evidence, so no new trial. I'm very sorry. Sometimes the justice system isn't fair. I know you're innocent but have no way to prove it. I will keep in touch.
Randy

The lawyer thought she was innocent! His opinion meant more than Diane's and the other prisoners', didn't it? Maybe I wasn't the kid of a murderer. I looked at the lawyer's letterhead. It had his phone number. The letter was dated May 1995. Fifteen years ago, but what the heck. I hesitated, then punched in the numbers.

A woman answered. She asked my name and, to my surprise, put me through.

"Hello."

"Mr. Webb, I hope I'm not bothering you, but you were my mother's lawyer years ago…"

"Who's this?"

"Carol Allan's daughter."

"It's Amanda?"

"Uh, yeah…"

"I'm so sorry. I heard about her… passing. She was a class act."

I took that in for a second. "I hope you don't mind—I wanted to ask you something."

He didn't interrupt to tell me he was too busy.

"I know it was a long time ago. But— why did the jury convict her?"

"Oh. That *was* a long time ago." He paused and I half expected him to beg off. But then he went on.

"I was straight out of law school, just finished articling. She called me first because we went to high school together."

"You did?"

"She couldn't afford a real lawyer." He smirked into the phone. "She was assigned a legal-aid lawyer who didn't give a crap. I worked with him, but it was hopeless. She lost because I didn't know what I was doing and the real lawyer didn't care."

"So she didn't do it?"

"Evidence was circumstantial. The steak knife was like a million others made in China and sold by Canadian Tire. Every house had a set just like it."

"Well then...?"

"The jury didn't like her. She wasn't soft like some women. She came across gutsy, didn't apologize for herself. They misread her."

It was a lot to take in. I didn't know what to say, so I didn't say anything.

"Look, my secretary's preparing some estate documents for you. Why don't you come by in a few days to pick them up? We'll talk."

* * *

I didn't know what to think. My mother was a convicted killer, but people close to her believed she was innocent. How could I form an opinion if I never knew her?

I leaned back on the couch and noticed the 1984 flyer for the band. The name at the bottom of the page was Iggy Bosco. He'd remember her. Maybe he could tell me something. Shouldn't be hard to find a guy with a name like that.

I typed *Iggy Bosco* into Google. Most of what came up was old stuff about the band. Vandal Boss had been big twenty-five years ago. They put their last names together to come up with Vand-al Boss. There was a lot about Freddy's murder. The headlines read, *Wife Convicted of Killing Freddy Allan. Gets Life*. Everyone agreed—she killed him because he couldn't keep it in his pants. The next-door neighbor (it didn't give her name), said she heard fighting whenever Freddy was back in town.

One article began:

After being dropped at home by a band member, it appeared that Mr. Allan was surprised by his attacker when he entered the house. Friends told police he usually partied pretty hard after a performance. The prosecution said Carol Allan, insane with jealousy, lay in wait for her husband to come home. While her three-year-old daughter slept in an upstairs bedroom—(that was me, the three-year-old!)—*Ms. Allan waited until her husband walked in the door then stabbed him to death with a kitchen knife. The defense lawyer argued the knife was identical to all the steak knives in the neighborhood. Since it had no fingerprints on it, there was no proof it had come from Ms. Allan's kitchen or that she was the killer. But the jury…*

I couldn't read any more, my hands were shaking.

Finally I found one little item about Iggy Bosco that was more current. It said he taught drums in a music store in the east end.

CHAPTER THREE

I took the subway farther east on Bloor than I'd ever been. Long past the stop I usually got off at to go home. No, not home anymore. The house I grew up in. Shelley's house on Maple Glen. All those years I was growing up she knew the whole story. She'd have to be in a cave to miss those headlines. I could understand why she didn't tell me when I was a kid. But I was twenty-three! It was a crappy family history, but it was *my* family history.

A weak October sun was shining when I climbed up to the street. My old neighborhood was nothing special, but it was the lap of luxury compared to this part of town. Some people sat on kitchen chairs outside the local coffee hangout. They watched me walk by. Two guys and a girl, all of them dressed by Goodwill.

I kept going along the main drag until I found it. Right next to a vegetable market. Painted on the glass storefront of the music shop: *Drum Lessons by Iggy Bosco of Vandal Boss*.

I opened the door and stepped into shadow. The dark wooden walls sucked in most of the light from the front window. A distant rumble came from upstairs. Someone going at the drums. A young dude in a plaid shirt stood behind the counter. He looked me over. I was wearing my little poofy skirt and jean jacket with high-heeled boots, so I knew I made an impression.

"I'm looking for Iggy Bosco."

His face fell as if I'd let him down. Must've thought I was a groupie. He glanced up at the wall clock. "With a student. Be down in ten minutes."

Dude would've been cute if he combed his hair. I stepped over to a display of guitars on the wall. The old wooden floor was worn smooth and creaked as I moved. I knew the dude's eyes were scanning my butt.

My mouth watered at the guitars, but the prices were way out of my range. I taught myself to play on a cheap second-hand one I found on Craigslist years ago. Had kind of a tinny sound, but I loved its little heart.

Footsteps came down behind the wall. A gawky kid stepped through a door across from the counter. An old guy with a pony-tail followed, carrying some sheet music. The kid disappeared out the front door.

"Someone to see you," said the counter dude.

I recognized Iggy from the picture. Same thin nose and owlish eyes. He'd gained weight and let his brown-gray hair grow too long.

He turned to me. "What can I do for ya?"

I suddenly got tongue-tied. This guy was a real musician! I didn't meet a lot of those in the hair salon.

"I…Could I talk to you? In private." Counter dude didn't need to know my business.

Iggy's eyebrow lifted with interest, and I realized he'd gotten the wrong impression. Old geezer. I followed him up the dark stairs, hoping I wouldn't have to fight him off. I'd been in that position before.

He led me into a room dominated by a drum set, and we were alone. "So, you a fan?" he said, standing too close. "Want some drum lessons? An autograph?"

I blurted out, "I'm Freddy's girl." That sounded strange even to me. To him, too, apparently.

"What?"

"Freddy Allan was my dad."

His mouth dropped open. Then he smiled, and his whole face lit up. He put one hand on my shoulder at arm's length. "Let's take a look at you! Freddy's kid! Can hardly believe it." He paused, a touch of sadness pulling down the smile a bit. "You grew up real nice. Got Freddy's chin." He tapped mine playfully.

I grinned, exhilarated.

"Sit down, sit down." He pointed me to a chair. "Mandy, right?"

I bobbed my head and sat down. "I don't know if you heard, but my mother—Carol—died last week."

His smile dissolved. "Man, I'm sorry. I didn't know. Lost touch." He looked away, embarrassed. "I visited her for a few years. Then…well, you know how it is, life moves on. You look a lot like her."

He studied my face. "She was the prettiest girl in school."

"You went to the same school?"

"You didn't know. Sure, how could you? We all went to the same school. Freddy and me and Carol. And Stu. Can't forget about Stu. Even if he's forgotten us."

"What was she like then?"

"Carol? Oh, she was a pistol. Real smart. Played a mean piano."

"She played piano?"

"She rocked! She wanted to teach music. All the guys in class were into her. She could've had any of us. She picked Freddy. No accounting for taste." He winked at me.

Iggy Bosco was joking with me. I swallowed.

"We were always touring. She played piano for us at the beginning. Freddy had to behave himself then. Girls liked him. Hell, they liked all of us, don't get me wrong. Never a shortage of groupies."

"He fooled around?"

"Couldn't help himself. All these chicks offering themselves up. He had this shyness about him—girls loved it."

"Carol knew?"

"No avoiding it. They were in her face when she was there. And when she wasn't...Well, when the cat's away, the mice will play. He didn't deny himself. If a chick went after him, he caved."

I looked down at the floor, trying not to hate my father.

"Don't feel bad. He was a kid himself. What was he? Twenty-two? He didn't want to grow up. Then they had you, and Carol had to grow up. It scared the hell out of him. She taught piano at a private school when she could."

"She stayed home to take care of me?"

Iggy smiled. "She was crazy about you."

I took a deep breath. "You think she killed him?"

"I would've. He had it coming."

"But do you think *she* did?"

"It was her knife."

"They never proved that. It was one of those steak knives made in China that everybody has. No fingerprints."

"Whatever." He shrugged. "She loved him. Chicks do strange things for love."

"Were you at the trial?"

He nodded, his face vacant, remembering. "She never had a chance. She didn't know it though. Head high. Looking confident. Always said she didn't do it. But then the jury guy read out 'Guilty!' Should've seen her face. She was stunned. We were all in shock when they took her out."

We both sat quiet a moment. I spoke to break the awkwardness. "You ever wonder how things would've gone if Freddy had lived? The band could've made it big."

"Hell no! That night was going to be our last anyway. We were breaking up."

"What...?"

"Couldn't last. Freddy and Stu were fighting over rights to the music. Freddy wanted to take Stu's name off the copyright because Freddy was the one who wrote all the songs. Well, Stu ain't one to lay down and play dead, if you've noticed."

I could hear a touch of envy in his voice. Stu was the only one who'd become a star.

"They fought over girls too. These groupies, they weren't fussy. They thought nothing of sleeping with Stu, then Freddy. Didn't make for peace on the road."

"You think Stu might've killed Freddy?"

He gave me a thoughtful look. "Jury said Carol did it."

"What if she didn't?"

"Seriously?"

"I'm trying to figure it out. But I need some information. Tell me about Stu. Was he mad enough to kill Freddy?"

"Look, Stu's a jerk, but he's no killer. Yeah, sure they fought. We were together night and day. But Carol and Freddy fought too. She was tall for a girl, like you. And she had more cause."

I ignored that last bit. "I need to talk to Stu. You know how to reach him?" I put a self-assurance in my voice I didn't feel.

"Stu? He's not so easy to get hold of. Always touring."

I took a breath, worked up some confidence. "I'm going to talk to the police about my mother. She's the only one they investigated. I'm going to tell them they should've looked at Stu. If he calls me before that— maybe he can explain himself."

I handed Iggy one of the cards from the salon with my number.

"He doesn't scare easy," Iggy said, squinting at me. He looked worried. Good.

CHAPTER FOUR

When I got home I sat down with my laptop and went on YouTube. I punched in *Vandal Boss*. Only one video came up, dated 1986. The year I was born. The clip was annoyingly dark and grainy. Only clear thing was Stu Van Dam, center stage, his big hair sprayed in place. He gyrated to the music—lyrics incomprehensible—in tight striped pants and a white ruffled shirt. He looked like he was eating the mike, in love with himself.

Then I saw Freddy. I couldn't believe it. This was my dad! He stood on the left in shadow, really into playing his guitar. He swayed some to the rhythm, but there was a stillness to him. His dark curly hair covered part of his face. He looked like a kid, though he must've been twenty-two. He leaned forward toward the mike and began to sing backup. That was when he looked up into the camera and my heart dropped. His eyes were sad and dreamy and so young! His face tilted toward the mike as he sang, his posture graceful. Especially compared to Stu who flailed his arms around like a deranged puppet. I could see the draw for all those chicks. Why they all went for Freddy. It was the eyes. His eyes said, *The world is too sad. Come with me.* Tears slipped down my cheeks. I wished I could remember him.

I played the video over again. This time I made out Iggy to the right in a headband. He was knocking on those drums with everything he had.

When it was over, I just sat there, drained. Who had killed Freddy? My mother? A jealous boyfriend? Did it really matter? Whoever it was, I'd been robbed of my family. Okay, it mattered.

YouTube listed related videos on the right of the screen. Usually that was annoying. Not this time. One thumbnail showed Stu Van Dam alone, singing his hit song. It was dated 1993. I clicked on it. He'd grown his hair down to his shoulders and dyed it blond. Yuck. Taking the mike with him, he jumped around the stage like Mick Jagger, sticking out his lips. The guy was gross, but it was hard not to watch him in his tight pants and shirt open to the navel. He was singing "Playgirl," the hit that had made him a star. I grew up listening to it, so I knew the words. I mouthed them as I watched the gymnastics on the screen.

You came along and broke my heart
Playgirl, playgirl.
Without even trying, right from the start
Playgirl, playgirl.
When you trapped me
When you smacked me
I loved you just the same.
I never knew I could be so true
And happy in my pain.

It was catchy and I couldn't get it out of my head over supper. I felt lazy—made some Kraft Dinner. My cell phone rang. I looked at the ID. It was Shelley. I didn't answer it.

* * *

Next day at the salon I was distracted. All I could think about was that I'd missed out on my real life. If only Shelley had told me about my mother, I could've gone to see her. The morning whizzed by. Good thing my hands knew how to cut hair all by themselves. A regular customer, Trish, chatted to me while I flatironed her bangs.

Suddenly there was a commotion at the front of the shop. My station was near the back so I couldn't see much. Everyone around me began to rush forward. Trish was stuck because I had her hair in my flatiron. Her eyes strained sideways in the mirror, trying to see. The crowd at the front were hooting and whistling. I had too much on my mind to care.

Then the crowd parted as if Moses was coming through. And everyone turned around to look at me. Someone was coming through, but it wasn't Moses. It was Stu Van Dam. I barely recognized him in jeans and a T-shirt, looking almost normal except for the platinum blond hair cut short and spiky. Taller than he looked in the video. He was heading right for me. My pulse quickened. Should I be scared? I guess he couldn't kill me in front of all these people.

Trish's mouth hung open as he approached.

My boss, Tony, shoved a pad of paper in front of him. "Could I have your autograph?"

Stu smiled and graciously signed.

"It's an honor to have you in our salon. Can I get you anything?"

"Nah, I'm good. I'm looking for Mandy."

Everyone stared at me.

Stu broke away and stopped in front of me. "I'd know you anywhere. Can we talk?"

One of the stylists jumped in and took the flatiron out of my hand. "I'll finish. You go ahead."

Everyone watched as I led him to the side door. He turned around and waved. Everyone cheered. He knew how to milk an audience. Probably too smart to do anything to me here. He followed me downstairs to our lunch room, the only private spot in the place. We sat down at the table. He'd gotten older, gained some weight but was tall enough to carry it. I was glad for the mirrors; I could keep a closer eye on him.

"You look just like your mother," he said with a sad smile. "Sorry about Carol. Iggy told me."

I nodded my thanks. "He said you were touring."

"Yeah, up at Casino Rama. Those old lady gamblers are really into me."

Not the tour I imagined.

"I hear you've been asking about me."

So here it was. I was on to something if he rushed from Ontario cottage country to see me. What was he scared of?

"I'm trying to figure out who killed Freddy. Maybe my mother was innocent."

"Go for it."

"I think someone close to my father might've killed him. Someone in the band."

45

He roared with laughter. "Don't beat around the bush or anything. Is that what this is about? You're kidding, right? Why would I kill Freddy?"

"He wanted to take your name off the songs."

His smile disappeared. "Yeah, well, Freddy had a big ego. He didn't get that I rearranged his songs every time I sang them. I'm an artist. I don't just sing the songs."

I caught him admiring himself in the mirror behind me. "So he never got a chance to take off your name, did he? The songs are still in both names?"

"Wake up, kid. Nobody gives a shit about those songs."

"You get the royalties for them, don't you?"

He smirked. "The royalties don't even pay for my sound crew."

I didn't know whether to believe him. "I heard you fought over girls."

"Iggy been spilling his guts? Look, it was nothing. They were groupies. Dime a dozen. I had my regular girl. She was always waiting for me."

Iggy hadn't mentioned her. "What happened to her?"

"Nothing happened to her. She's alive and kicking. I didn't kill her." He grinned at me and my suspicions mellowed. But he was a good actor.

"Why didn't you marry her?"

"How d'you know I didn't?" He fixed his platinum spikes in the mirror. "Yeah, you're right. I'm not the marrying kind. Never home. She understands. But I did right by her. Set her up in her own club. Maybe you been there? Brooke's."

I'd heard of it. Cool place.

"You tell her I sent you and she won't shut up about me. Great chick."

"If you're innocent, why'd you come as soon as you heard I was asking about you?"

He tilted his great blond head forward, like he was going to tell me a secret. "Wanted to see who was making trouble. You start rumors, sometimes things can get ugly. Wouldn't want that, would we?"

I sat back in my chair as if he'd poked me in the eye.

CHAPTER FIVE

That night I dressed carefully. Though I wanted to be a musician I didn't get out to clubs much. Especially not cool clubs where the floor didn't smell of beer.

I liked to dress down. God forbid people should think I cared enough to dress up for them—it was a hangup of mine. If you don't care, you don't get hurt, right? But there were different ways to dress down, and this time it had to be funky.

I stared at the clothes in my closet. The poofy skirt? Too young, unless I wanted to get carded. The mini-dress? Maybe.

I tended to dress from the shoes up. If I was going to wear my sexy high-heeled motorcycle boots, the outfit would have to go with them. What impression did I want to make? It was important because one day I might want to come back to the place and bring my guitar. Yes, I had to speak to Stu's squeeze to see if he was telling anywhere near the truth. (Because he sure didn't seem the reliable type.) But no reason I couldn't check the place out.

So I pulled on some black leggings, threw over my purple plaid mini-dress and topped it with a little jean jacket. I straightened the curls out of my hair with a flatiron, then sprayed it till it wouldn't move. At least I had control over *something*. I was ready.

Guys on the subway checked me out. I was used to that even when I wasn't all dolled up. I usually liked it, though I never let on. Now I was too riled up thinking about what I would do when I got to the club. I rode west into the Annex.

It was dark by the time I got to street level. I walked past cute little shops with handmade jewelry and clothes designed by the owner. People sat outside on the patio of an Italian restaurant under a striped awning. Looked like everybody was having a good time. I was cool with that. I just wished *I* was having a good time. Brooke's was in a building on a corner, the name lit up in big orange letters over the front door.

I didn't feel it, but I knew that confidence was everything. So I held up my head and walked like I knew where I was going. I opened the door to Brooke's and stepped inside, my heart loud in my ears.

I'd arrived early so I wouldn't have to compete with the music. As usual in a club, the lighting was low. But this place sparkled—the bottles behind the bar to the right, the wall sconces, the shiny wood floor.

A guy with a shaved head stood behind the bar wiping glasses.

"I'm looking for Brooke," I said.

"Through that door." He pointed to one side. "Office on your left."

I opened the door to a short hall. In front of me, a staircase marked *Private* led to the second floor. A door to the left said *Office*. On the right a wider door tempted me. I opened that one a crack and saw a large room set with round wood tables. A girl and three guys were setting up on the low stage at the front. One day, I thought, that might be me.

I headed toward the office door. I knocked and was surprised when it opened. A pretty auburn-haired woman stood there watching me. Not young, but hot.

"Can I help you?"

She was wearing jeans and a long turquoise shirt cinched at the waist with a leather belt.

"I'm looking for Brooke."

"That's me," she said, waiting in the door.

"I wanted to talk to you about Freddy Allan."

Her eyes grew wide.

"He was my father."

Her jaw dropped, and then she flung the door open. She grabbed both my hands. "Freddy's little girl! I can't believe it." She studied my face. "You grew up so pretty. You have his eyes."

I wondered at this, since his eyes seemed so sad in the picture. But I was pleased, and felt myself go red.

She pulled me into the room and sat me down in a chair opposite her. "So tell me about yourself. What're doing these days?"

I hadn't expected this reaction. "I'm styling hair right now, but I want to get into music." I'd never said that out loud to anyone besides Shelley. Was kind of afraid to say it. What if it never happened?

"Well, like father, like daughter," she said. "When you have something, I'd love to hear it."

My heart skipped. "Wow! That's awesome! Better get practicing." I waved in the direction of the door. "You have an amazing place here. Stu told me about it. He said to come."

Her expression changed, the smile suddenly forced. "When did you talk to Stu?"

"Uh, well…" Did she know he was in town? I didn't want to be the cause of trouble between them. "I wanted to talk to him about my dad. I heard they were fighting at the end."

She looked away, embarrassed. Must've had her own secrets. "Yeah, well, two guys with hormones. They were together all the time. Mostly on a bus. No surprise they were fighting."

"Does Stu have a temper? Is he violent?"

"What're you asking?"

"How mad was he? Mad enough to kill?"

She stared at me. "Carol killed Freddy. Everyone knew that." Then she softened. "I know she was your mother, and it's hard to accept…"

"What if she didn't do it? What if someone else killed him?"

She took in a breath. "Whatever gets you through the night."

"I just need to know."

"Well, it wasn't Stu. He's big and loud, but he'd never hurt anybody."

"Were you there, that last night?"

"Sure."

"What happened after the show?"

"Same thing as always. We all went back to the dressing room. They brought in some food. After we ate, we did some drugs. The guys were so wired at the end of a gig they needed something to get off on. I only smoked weed. They were into the hard stuff."

"Freddy too?"

"Course."

"Then what?"

"After a while we all passed out. Not too glamorous."

"When did Freddy leave?"

"Don't remember."

"Did you and Stu leave together?"

She took a breath. "Some little groupie found us and started telling him how great he was. He lapped it up. I took off, mad."

"So he could've followed Freddy home."

"Look, he was too wasted to kill anyone. He could hardly walk."

I sat back in the chair. If that was true, Stu wasn't my guy. I was disappointed and relieved at the same time.

"Did you know my mother?"

She blinked at my change of direction. "Yeah. She was cool. She changed when she had you. Got serious. Looked out for you."

"And you really think she killed Freddy?"

Brooke shrugged. "He hurt her. People do strange things when they're hurt."

I thought about that. "Maybe he hurt someone else. Was there anyone else mad enough to kill him?"

She pursed her lips. "Well, come to think of it—there was this girl. She sang with the band that opened for them. Toured together. What was her name? Jill. It was a long time ago. Let me think. Jill Hanes. She was intense. She had a thing for Freddy. Threw herself at him. He never refused. But he didn't stay with any girl for long. All hell broke loose when he broke it off."

"You know where she is now?"

"I heard she's living in public housing. St. Jamestown, I think. You know, the one that's always on the news."

There was a light tap at the door, then it opened partway. A cute dark-haired dude stuck his head in.

"Hey, Mom, they're asking for you."

Brooke's cheeks flushed. "I'll be right there."

The door closed. I pasted a smile on my face to cover up my surprise.

"I didn't know you had kids," I said sweetly.

"Just one. Lexy. He helps me run the place."

She stood up, in a hurry to go. "Oh, if you're going looking for Jill, watch yourself there. Not the safest place."

CHAPTER SIX

I hustled to get my late-morning client finished before lunch. I was fast, not slack, so her hair still looked cool. I had an hour and a half to go before my next client. Time enough to find Jill Hanes. St. Jamestown was on the subway line I took to get home. I never got off there. For obvious reasons.

I took off the white skirt and blouse that was my hairdresser's uniform. I didn't want to stand out in that part of town. If I blended in, maybe the locals wouldn't bother me. I pulled on a T-shirt and jeans and the scruffy old jean jacket I'd brought from home.

It was a ten-minute subway ride from the salon. I'd found Jill's address in the white pages online. Just not the apartment number.

Even from a distance the place creeped me out. It was a forest of high-rises, a dozen cement slabs pushing up into the sky. I passed three of the ugly blocks before finding Jill's. There were two guys I didn't like the look of hanging out on the other side of the street. They stood there smoking, trying to look all tough. They squinted at me like they were inspectors and I was meat. I ignored them and hurried into the building.

There were some names scribbled on a piece of paper taped to the wall just inside; some had apartment numbers. Maybe Jill's was there, maybe not. A big old guy was standing with his back against the wall, so I couldn't read the names. He wore a heavy jacket and dirty gray tuque like it was still winter.

"Five bucks if you want in," he said. Booze on his breath.

He was big but he was old. And hammered. If I pushed him, he would fall down. "Hey," I said, "what's that?" I pointed to the ceiling.

He moved away from the wall to look up, and I found Jill's name and apartment number scrawled on the paper.

He grabbed my arm as I tried to step past. He was stronger than I thought. So was the smell. Unwashed skin and sweat. I looked in his red-rimmed eyes. They were blank.

"Gimme five bucks."

If he knocked me down to the cement floor, my head could split open.

"Let go of me or I'll call the cops."

I reached into my purse with my free hand and brought out my cell.

He grunted and let go. I ran inside.

The elevator smelled like piss. I took it up to Jill's floor and wandered down the hall past the graffiti. Someone had spray-painted an exclamation mark as big as me on the wall. I got that. Life was full of surprises. It felt strange meeting these people who knew my dad. I wasn't sure I liked him. It sucked, finding out my real dad wasn't such a great guy.

I found her apartment number and knocked on the door. I heard kids shouting and dishes clattering inside. I knocked again. Finally the door swung open. A large chick (okay, she was fat) stood there, one hand on a humungous hip. Long brown hair pulled off her face in a headband.

"I said come after lunch. I'm busy now." She started to close the door in my face.

"I'm looking for Jill Hanes."

She held the door open a crack. "You're not a cop?" She looked me up and down, nervous now. Yelling inside got louder. "Shut up!" she barked behind her.

"I'm Freddy Allan's kid. I wanted to talk to Jill about him."

She opened the door wide and smiled. "You're kidding. Freddy Allan's girl? That's a name I haven't heard in a long time."

The phone rang in another room. She waved at me to follow as she waddled into the kitchen and picked up the phone.

"Yeah, I got it," she said into the receiver. "Give me half an hour."

Three little kids sat at a table, getting orange SpaghettiOs all over their mouths.

"Grandma!" one said. "I want chocolate cake for dessert."

The others piped in, "Me too!"

Jill bent toward them in a threatening pose. They kept eating, unfazed. "Listen up! I'm going into the other room with this lady, and I don't want to hear squat out of any of you."

They stared at me, their mouths moving. It was weird to be called a lady. I still felt like a kid. But they were three or four years old, so to them I was a lady. With a start, I thought: I was around their age when my world fell apart.

Jill led me into the living room. Toys everywhere. Dolls and stuffed bears and plastic tea cups all over the dirty carpet. I moved a sticky rubber dinosaur to sit down on the tattered sofa.

"So, you're Freddy's kid." She tilted her head, watching me. "I can see the resemblance. He was a great guy. Terrible what happened to him."

"I heard you two were…going out."

"Oh." She looked down. "I guess it was no secret. Yeah, I was crazy about him." Then she studied me like she was trying to find him in my face. "We toured together. I would've done anything for him. I was a kid. I thought he loved me."

I tried to picture Jill young and thin. "He broke it off?"

She looked away. "One day he just said there was somebody else. He said I deserved better! What a line. Just like that. I was young, he said, and I'd find the right guy. But I didn't want the right guy. I wanted *him*."

I nodded to be polite. "Were you there that last night?"

"You mean when...?" She nodded. "We shared a cab home—he was so wasted. The whole way I tried to persuade him he loved me. I don't think he heard a word."

"Then what happened?"

"We stopped in front of his house and he got out. Never saw him again."

"You were angry he dumped you."

"Sure..."

"Angry enough to...?"

"Just what're you getting at?" Her face went red. "Man, you've got nerve, girl.

I didn't have to let you in here. You got no right...Besides, everyone knew Carol did it."

The phone rang. She picked up the handset beside her. "Yeah, it just came in," she said, turning away from me. "Same terms as usual." She hung up.

"What if she didn't do it?"

"What? Oh. Look, I don't know what she told you."

"She died last week."

She tilted her head. "That's tough." She pursed her lips. "Doesn't change anything. Why would I kill him? I loved him."

"People do funny things when they're hurt." So maybe that was true. "He was leaving you for another chick."

"That was his story. Could've been giving me a line."

I was running around in circles. "You and the cab driver were the last ones to see him alive. Did the cops talk to you?"

"Yeah. They wanted to know if I saw anything. Maybe another car. Someone hanging around. They asked the cabbie too."

"Did you see anything?"

"I was so mad I couldn't see straight. Freddy got out of the car, and I told the cabbie to burn rubber. Wasn't in a state to notice anything."

"What about the cabbie?"

She shook her head. "You're wasting your time, honey. She did it."

Someone knocked at Jill's door. I jumped.

She heaved herself off the couch. "He was right about one thing," she said. "I deserved better." She waved at the shabby sofa and chairs. "Never got it. Just a daycare and mouths to feed. Nobody looking out for me but me."

It was time to take off. I still needed my job.

I got up, wondering if Jill had told me the truth or if she was a good liar.

When she opened the door, two big guys with tattoos stood there. "Hey, Jill, baby, whatcha got for us today?"

She let them inside, and we all stared at each other.

"I do some business on the side," she said to me, nervous again. "Key chains."

I nodded. Couldn't care less what she was dealing.

I mumbled my goodbyes and slunk past them out the door.

"Hey, Jill, who's your friend?"

She closed the door and I headed for the elevator. I was so out of there.

CHAPTER SEVEN

The lawyer's secretary had called and said the papers for the estate were ready. So after work, I changed into my knock-off designer jeans and touched up my hair and makeup. I'd never been to a lawyer's office before.

I took the subway downtown to King Street, then walked east a few blocks. It looked like one of those sketchy neighborhoods that artists made funky, and while it was still cheap, the developers moved in. New condos were going up behind boards.

Upscale furniture stores beside shops selling cigarettes and hot dog buns.

When I got to the street number, I stopped, surprised. It was a storefront. I'd pictured something different. Something more private up some stairs in an office building. At least the blinds were closed inside the window and you couldn't see in. *Randall Webb, Law Office* was painted in small block letters on the glass.

I opened the door and walked in. The reception desk was piled neatly with folders. Some chairs sat near the window. A door behind the desk was open, leading to another room. A man was talking on the phone in the invisible distance. I headed over.

Once at the door, I got shy and just stood there. Randall Webb was leaning back in his leather chair behind a desk. Not what I expected. Thinning brown hair, kind of long for a lawyer pushing fifty. The sleeves of his white shirt rolled up.

"Look, there's not much more I can do," he was saying into the phone. "They're cracking down on drunk drivers these days…"

Webb looked up and saw me. Without missing a beat, he waved for me to sit down in a chair in front of the desk. He got rid of the guy on the phone and stood up.

He gave me a big smile. "You're Carol's kid, aren't you? I'd know you anywhere." He came around the desk and put out his hand.

I took it shyly. He sat down in a chair beside me. Clean jeans. High-top runners.

"She was a beauty. You look just like her."

I smiled like a dork.

"We were kids when we met. Grade ten."

"Seriously?"

"I had a crush on her. But she was in love with Freddy from day one."

"Then you knew my father too?"

He grinned. "Skinny little guy."

"And you knew the other dudes in the band."

"Iggy and Stu, yeah. They were the cool guys. I was the nerd. I did my homework. They played music. The rest is history."

For a second I was irritated with my mother. She could've picked anyone and she picked Freddy. Then it dawned on me that I wouldn't be here if she hadn't.

"You were just a kid when…You don't remember anything, do you?"

I shook my head.

"Lucky," he said. He smiled sadly. "You were real cute. A neighbor was looking after you when I got there. Then Child Welfare came in. It broke Carol's heart to give you up. No shortage of offers for you. She asked me to sort it out."

"You arranged for my adoption?"

He fixed his eyes on me, searching. "I hope it worked out."

I didn't want to make him feel bad. I shrugged. "Yeah. Sure." Wasn't his fault I didn't get along with Shelley.

"You got some money coming when the paperwork's done. Mostly from the sale of the house."

"House?"

"Don't remember that either, eh? She asked me to sell it. The money paid for her legal fees. Appeals. None of it helped." He shrugged. "There's a good chunk left. It'll take awhile for you to get it." He looked at me like he was sorry. "I'll send you a statement, so you can see what's what."

Then he smiled again. "Got something for you." He pointed to the floor behind him. "It's been cluttering up my office."

He got up and ducked into a corner behind his desk. When he stood up, he was carrying a leather guitar case.

"It was your father's. Carol kept it all these years."

I jumped up, tingling all over. He put the case down on his chair. I just stood there staring.

"Go on," he said. "Open it."

I flicked open the latch and raised the cover. The light hit the shiny wood. A *Gibson*! The best guitar in the world. And even better: my father had played it. I lifted it in my arms like a baby.

"You play?" he asked.

I smiled and nodded, plucking the strings. It was out of tune.

"Hey, Mr. Webb!" Someone was in the front office.

A man poked his head in the door. "Gotta talk to you, Mr. Webb. Cops said I violated parole. That's bull! All I did was stick a note under her door…"

Webb stayed calm, must've been used to this kind of interruption. "I told you not to contact her. That means no note, no phone call, *nada*. Wait outside."

"I love her, man. I'd never hurt her."

Webb walked over to the door and put his hand on the dude's shoulder. "I'll be with you shortly. Wait outside."

While he was busy, I noticed some papers lying in the guitar case. I put the Gibson down carefully on my chair and picked through the sheets. It was music, some with notes written by hand.

Webb freed himself from the guy and came back into the room.

"Did you meet Diane?" he asked. "She said she was bringing you some of Carol's stuff."

I nodded. "You know Diane too?"

"Just on the phone. Never met her. Carol talked about her when I came to visit. I was glad she'd made a friend who wasn't in for murder."

I was confused. "Diane looked after her in the infirmary."

"Yeah. I guess she got brownie points for that. Maybe it was her get-out-of-jail card."

"Diane was a prisoner?"

"She tell you otherwise?"

"She said she was a nurse."

"Maybe in some other life. I wouldn't want her to nurse me. She's a con artist. Bilked old ladies out of their savings."

CHAPTER EIGHT

I could hardly see straight going home, I was so mad. People on the subway kept their distance. Must've had smoke coming out of my ears. I hugged the guitar case like there was a machine gun inside. I wished. That jailbird Diane really conned me. I'd fallen for her story, all of it. If she lied about who she was, what else did she lie about? She was one of the people who claimed my mother was innocent. Was it any less true if Diane was a liar?

I shivered and stared out the window of the subway. We were speeding through the black tunnel. If my mother was a killer, this was where my life would stay—in a dark tunnel. I thought back on everyone I'd talked to who knew her. They all believed she was guilty.

I had to speak to Diane again. Get the truth this time. I'd shake her until she coughed it up. What did I do with the scrap of paper she'd written her address on? I prayed it was on the coffee table at home where she'd left it.

I lugged the guitar up the stairs of the subway and down the street. It was heavy, but I loved every inch of it. Had to be careful not to bang it in the elevator to the third floor. I was panting when I finally put it down on the rug in my living room.

I rushed to the coffee table. Diane's note was right there on top of one of my hairstyling magazines. Place wasn't far. Cabbagetown. There was a phone number. But I wasn't going to call. Then she could bolt and avoid me. I'd take my chances she was home. If not, I'd wait.

I checked the clock in my tiny kitchen. Nearly eight. My stomach was growling. What did I eat today? Not much. I threw some cheese between two slices of whole-wheat bread. I scarfed it down, grabbed a chocolate bar and ran out the door.

After a couple of subway stops, I was there in fifteen minutes. The street Diane was staying on was not the best. Not the worst either. I passed a lot of old houses with drooping porches. Then I found it. A big Victorian number, not quite falling down.

The front door was unlocked, but then I was stuck in a small hall with numbers and push buttons on the wall. And a locked door. I pressed the bell for her apartment, number 204. No answer. So either she wasn't home, or she didn't want visitors. I wasn't giving up that easy.

I pushed someone else's bell. Some dude answered. I said in my sweetest voice, "I forgot my key. Could you please unlock the door?"

"Who's this?" he asked.

"Diane," I said.

The buzzer rang and I opened the door. Nice guy. Too trusting though.

I climbed up a dark wooden staircase to the second floor. I knocked on 204. Nothing. Maybe there were people she didn't want to see. Like one of those old ladies she'd swindled.

"Diane! It's me. Amanda."

Dead quiet. So maybe she didn't want to see me either. Now what? I wasn't going to be a pussy and slink away. I banged on the door. I was going to stand up for myself.

"Diane! Open up!"

I looked down the hall. Two more apartments. If I was disturbing anybody, they didn't come running.

I grabbed the doorknob and jiggled it around to let her know I meant business. The door opened! I stood there like an idiot. Well, I wasn't the only one. She wasn't too swift, leaving the door unlocked. Anybody could walk in.

I pushed the door open farther, waiting for her to screech. But it was dark inside. She wasn't home. I felt along the wall and turned on the light switch. Small tidy kitchen.

The living room was dark. I could wait for her there. I groped at a floor lamp in the shadow. Flicked it on.

I froze. She was lying on the sofa, out cold in her green scrubs. Her pageboy hair fell over her face.

"Diane?" I came closer. A rubber strip was tied around her arm above the elbow.

I felt sick to my stomach. I knew what the stuff on the coffee table was. A bent spoon, a lighter, a small vial of water, some cotton balls. The needle had dropped to the floor.

I bent over her. Touched her arm. Shook her a bit. "Diane?" I tried to find a pulse in her wrist. Either she didn't have one, or I was doing it wrong. Didn't really matter anyway. She was too cold to be alive. Crazy lady OD'd.

I stood up fast, my heart thumping. I'd never seen a dead body before. It was like a shell. The person inside was gone.

I used the cell on her coffee table to call 9-1-1. I gave the operator Diane's address and said I was pretty sure she was dead.

"Can I have your name please?" said the voice on the line.

I freaked out. I disconnected and dropped the phone like it was on fire. I had to get out of there. This had nothing to do with me. But the cops would jump to conclusions if they found me there. I couldn't do anything more for Diane.

I stuck my head into the hall to make sure it was empty. I was about to jump out the door, but something held me back. I turned around and tiptoed back into the living room. Like she was going to wake up.

I picked up her cell from the rug where it had fallen. My number was in it. The cops would roll through the list and find me. They'd put two and two together and come up with five.

I dropped the cell into my purse. Then I ran.

CHAPTER NINE

I took the side streets going home. Still freaking, I looked over my shoulder every other minute. As if someone was following. As if I was guilty of something. The only thing I was guilty of was bad timing. An hour earlier and the 9-1-1 call might've helped. Don't get me wrong— I was sorry Diane was dead. But all I could think of was that I couldn't ask her any more questions. I would never know any more about my mother.

When I got home, I took out the only bottle of liquor I owned. Peach brandy that Shelley gave me when I moved out. I instantly felt guilty. I'd been avoiding her calls. There was no one else I could talk to about this. I had to tell somebody.

I drank down a glass. Then I punched in her number.

"Hello?"

"It's me," I said.

Pause. "Hi, kid." Her voice had an edge to it. "What's up?"

"Something happened. Something terrible." I heard her breathe into the phone, waiting. "Diane, the one who told me about my mother—I mean my birth mother—she's dead! I found her lying there. I called nine-one-one. I was so scared…"

"Slow down! When was this?"

"Fifteen minutes ago! I just got home. I'm still shaking."

"That's horrible. What did the police say?"

"I didn't wait around for them."

"Ambulance guys?"

"I called nine-one-one and took off. You think that was bad?" Suddenly she was my mother again.

"Probably the best thing, considering."

Yeah, considering my real mother died in prison.

"What were you doing there?"

"I wanted to talk to her. She knew Carol. I had some questions."

Hesitation. "You better leave all that behind you."

"I have to know the truth."

"It'll only hurt you."

"Why are you so sure? What if she didn't do it?"

She waited a few seconds. Then she said, "I've been around a lot longer than you. Trust me. Let it go."

"Trust you? You lied to me about the most important thing in my life. I'll never trust you again!"

I pushed the button to disconnect. I felt stupid right away. I was on edge and taking it out on her.

I poured myself another glass of peach brandy. It went down nice and warm.

I took the guitar out of the case and put it down on the sofa. I looked over the papers inside the case. Sheets of music. Some Vandal Boss songs I recognized. Shelley had an old boom box she used to play in the salon. Those funny little audio-tapes when I was a kid. I remembered hearing Vandal Boss songs for the first time when I came in to watch her cut hair. And here was their own sheet music! Notes in the margins, words underlined. Awesome!

Underneath the pile was a big envelope, no writing on it. I took out the one sheet of yellowed paper inside. It was one of those pages that already had the staff lines printed on it. The musical notes were printed

by hand. Not round like the printed ones.
These were just strokes with tails, like
someone going real fast to get it all down.
Then below each bar, lyrics in small tight
letters to fit them all in. At the top it said,
"Best Girl." In the bottom corner was a
signature: *Freddy Allan. For my best girl, Mandy.*

I just stared at it. My heart pounded.
Tears rolled down my face.

You came along and broke my heart
Best girl, best girl.
Without even trying right from the start
Best girl, best girl.
Now you're walking
Now you're talking
Girl, you're sweet as candy.
I never knew I could love so true
My own sweet baby Mandy.

For my best girl, Mandy. He loved me. My
dad loved me! All the bad things I heard

about him fell away. I read the words again through my tears.

Hey, wait! Those chords, those words—they were the lyrics from "Playgirl," Stu Van Dam's hit song. A couple of lines were different. The rest of the song was the same. I looked for Stu's name on the sheet. *Nada*. Then I saw the date below the signature. *December 3, 1990.* My birthday! My dad wrote it for my birthday. I was four years old. A month later he was gone.

A shiver ran down my back. Would Stu have killed him for a song? Not just any song. The song that made his career. I looked at the sheet, picking up the Gibson. I hummed it, then tried the rest of the notes. They went up and down in the same places as "Playgirl," but it was hard to tell. There were letters of the alphabet above the music notes. Guitar chords. I strummed the chords slowly and sang the words. Wow! Now I recognized it. Stu had improvised to fit the song to his voice. But it was the same song! Stu had stolen it from my dad.

I found the cell number Stu gave me when he came to the salon.

"Yo!" he answered.

"Stu?" I tried to control my anger. "It's Amanda."

"Yeah, babe. What's up?"

"I need to talk to you."

"Lucky break. Come to Brooke's tomorrow night. Rockin' new artist playing his first gig. You'll love it." He hung up.

I gritted my teeth.

CHAPTER TEN

The next day I photocopied the "Best Girl" sheet in the salon office. I kept myself calm the whole day, playing out what would happen that night. I would tell Stu I knew what he'd done. At first he'd deny it. Then I'd show him the photocopy. Finally he'd see that I had him. He'd confess. I would call the cops and they'd take him away. Okay, things probably wouldn't go quite that smoothly. But my mother's name would be cleared. I wouldn't be the kid of a murderer anymore.

Later that night, I changed into my knock-off designer jeans. They'd already seen my poofy skirt. Besides, I wanted them to take me seriously. I wanted to look grown-up. It's hard to do that in a poofy skirt.

Their rocking new star wouldn't go on till after ten, the usual club time. I wasn't interested in him, so I showed up at Brooke's with time to spare. I walked through the bar. No Stu. I went through the same door as last time and stepped into the hall. I knocked on the office door where I'd found Brooke before. No one home. I headed back the other way and opened the wide door toward the stage. Lexy and a few other guys were setting up for the show.

Without looking up, Lexy said, "Show's in an hour. Come back then."

I walked in, all confident. He was just a kid. "I was talking to your mom the other day, remember? Old family friend."

He looked up and blinked, some curly bangs in his face. "Oh. Yeah, sure."

"I'm looking for Stu."

"Upstairs," he said, giving me another quick look before going back to work. Probably wondering why his mom had never mentioned me.

I climbed the stairs, past the Private sign. I hesitated at the door. Maybe this wasn't such a smart idea. Stu was a big guy. If he didn't like what I had to say, he could knock me flat without trying. I took my cell phone out of my bag and held on to it. He might think twice if he thought the cops were on speed dial.

I wasn't going to wimp out. I could do this. I knocked.

Stu opened the door, blond hair freshly spiked. "Hey, babe. Glad you could make it. Come on in."

I took a breath and followed him, holding my cell in my hand. The place was decorated in expensive modern. White leather sofa. Abstract blue and white rug on the dark wood floor. Big-screen TV. Snazzy. Royalty money.

"Drink?" he asked, pouring one for himself at the bar. "Vodka? Tequila?"

I shook my head. Now that I was here, it was awkward. He was the star. I was the kid who cut hair for a living.

"Take a load off," he said, sitting down on the sofa. He looked at my hand. "Expecting a call?"

Good. He noticed. I reached into my handbag and brought out the folded photo-copy of "Best Girl." I walked toward him and handed it over.

"What's this?" he said, unraveling it. He sat still, his eyes taking it in. "Wow! This is ancient. Where'd you dig it up?"

"My mother kept it."

"No shit."

"Read the words," I said, sitting down on the edge of the sofa, nervous.

He stared at the page. His face went white.

"Look familiar?"

"Well…"

"It's 'Playgirl.' Everything's the same but a couple of lines."

"No, it can't be…"

"'Playgirl' is 'Best Girl.'"

"It's probably a coincidence. Freddy and me were close. On the same wavelength, you know?"

"You stole his song!"

"No! I —"

"You killed him for that song!"

Stu's mouth opened, then closed. He shook his head. "No! You got it all wrong." He closed his eyes. "He was already dead when I found it."

He rubbed his forehead as if it hurt. "Freddy kept a stash of songs in our van,

95

and I was cleaning it out after he…you know. Then I saw this piece and it was good. Not great, mind you. I gave it *style*. I rocked it out, man! I put my own stamp on it. This song would've gone nowhere without *me*."

He was so full of himself I wanted to smack him. "Here's what I think. You wanted the song so bad, you killed Freddy when he wouldn't give it to you."

He shook his big blond head. "If I'd sung it for him and he liked it, he would've played backup guitar for me. He wasn't stupid."

"Why should I believe you?"

"Because you're not stupid either. Look, how much do you want?"

I stared at him. "What do you mean?"

"How much will make you happy?"

"Are you trying to pay me off so I don't go to the cops?"

He laughed. His face went bright, made him look years younger. "*Go* to the cops.

I didn't do it. I know it hurts to think your mother did, but that's no reason to go around pointing fingers."

Is that what I was doing? Pointing fingers to deflect the guilt?

Just then Brooke walked into the room. She was trying to put on an earring, pushing away her thick auburn hair, when she saw me. "Oh! Hi. Come for the show?"

"I can't stay," I said, embarrassed, jumping up.

"Well, I'm just going down now— you might catch him rehearsing before he starts."

I threw back what I hoped was a meaningful look at Stu. Then I let Brooke lead me downstairs. When she opened the wide door to the club area, Lexy stood center stage playing his guitar, singing a folky rock song.

"Isn't he great?" she said, grinning at her son.

Lexy was the hot new artist! Thing was—the song kicked ass. He was good. He was also the owner's son, so he got a chance to prove it. The spotlight shone on him, his face turned toward his guitar while he checked the chords. That's when I saw it. His ear. It was a flat clamshell like mine. Clamshell ears! What were the odds of that? I watched the way he stood there, slumped over his guitar, like the world was too sad to look in the eye. The rhythmic way he moved his head, the dark hair falling over his face. I'd seen that before. The YouTube video. *Freddy*. I stared at him, stunned by the recognition. It was so obvious. I looked at Brooke. Brooke and Freddy?

"Can I talk to you?"

I pulled her out into the hall where we were alone.

"Is there something you want to tell me about Lexy?"

Her smile disappeared.

"I mean…is he…um…related to me?"

"What?"

"He doesn't look like Stu's kid."

"I don't know what you're talking about."

I pulled my hair back from my ear. She stared at it. "He's got ears like mine. Like Freddy's. He moves like Freddy."

Her face went pale and she looked away. "You're imagining things. Lexy is Stu's son."

"Doesn't Stu see he doesn't look like him?"

"Kids don't always look like their parents."

"No, sometimes they look like their parents' friends."

She gave me a dirty look.

"If I have a brother," I said, the word strange in my mouth, "I want to know."

"Stu's nuts about the kid. Been paying his keep the whole time. Don't go spreading rumors."

"Maybe that's a motive for murder," I said.

She pulled in a sudden breath. "There was no motive. Stu never found out. Hey, it was a mistake! Freddy and I were both at a low point and...But you're wrong about Stu. He may be a dick, but he wouldn't kill anybody. Look, if you want something, money—whatever...Just don't say anything. *Please.*"

Oh my god! I had a brother!

She gave me a long pleading look. I shrugged, numb. She went back into the club to join Lexy.

I stood there confused, angry. Everyone wanted to give me money. Why wasn't I grateful?

CHAPTER ELEVEN

That night I tossed and turned in bed for hours. All I could think was, *She did it*. My mother killed my father. I was the kid of a murderer. Shelley was right. It was better not to know the truth. Better not to feel this pain in my chest where my heart was supposed to be.

The whole time I had been on a wild-goose chase. Now it was over. There was no one else to pin the murder on, no one else who looked guilty. I felt like a chump for believing Diane. She didn't have to work hard to convince me my mother was innocent. I wanted desperately to believe her. But why did she bother? What did she get out of it?

By three in the morning I gave up on sleep. I turned on the light and sat up in bed. The envelope Diane had given me lay on my night table. I pulled out the shots of my parents. Stared at the one where they had their arms around each other. A young couple in love. Carol with her bright eyes and bushy hair, smiling at the camera, all innocent and happy. When did she become desperate enough to kill?

For the first time since I started working at the salon, I called in sick. I *felt* sick. I stayed in bed till noon. Then I stood in front of the mirror staring at myself in pajamas, my hair all over the place. I looked like her, everybody said so. Was I like her? Was I desperate?

I opened a can of chicken soup for lunch. Then I went back to bed.

The phone woke me up late in the afternoon. I looked at the caller ID. Shelley. I didn't answer, but I felt guilty enough to get up and dress. I was also getting hungry. I checked the fridge. I was hankering for a grilled cheese sandwich. Only I was out of cheese. Oh well, I had to go out. The local convenience store sold all the necessary food groups—coffee, sugar, cheese and bread. This was what I lived on.

It was good to get outside. The sun was still out, but it was cooling off. I picked up some coffee and cheese, and because I felt sorry for myself, a chocolate bar. I trudged home. Remembered to check my mailbox on the way in. Along with the usual junk mail, there was another letter from the lawyer.

I set my goodies down on the table and ripped open the envelope. It was a statement of money spent over the years, like he'd promised. Legal fees for the trial—modest because of legal aid. Legal fees for the appeal. Court costs. Photocopying costs. Costs for this, costs for that. Sale of the house, real estate fees, legal fees, taxes. On and on. My eyes glazed over.

This much I figured out: the house had sold for $120,000. He had subtracted the costs, then added bank interest over the years. There was $91,000 left! He said there would still be some expenses and he'd let me know the final figure. But wow! That was more money than I ever expected to see in one place. I didn't know whether to want the money or be creeped out by it. An inheritance from a killer.

I fried my grilled cheese sandwich and sat there chewing, not happy. Apart from the idea of blood money, something else bothered me. Something in the statement.

I set the letter in front of me and read as I ate. The house Carol sold. It was the address.

I started to cough. This was wrong. They had it at 140 Maple Glen. Somehow they had confused it with Shelley's house on Maple Glen. But that wasn't quite right either, because Shelley was at 142. Did the lawyer screw up? Did the secretary type in Shelley's address by mistake? But the house number was wrong.

I reached for my cell and called Randall Webb's office, hoping he was working late.

"Webb here," he answered.

"It's Amanda Moss. I think there's a mistake in the papers you sent me. The address of my mother's house— the one she sold. One forty Maple Glen. That's next door to where I grew up. Maybe it's a typo…"

"Oh. No mistake," he said. "The woman who adopted you lived next door. Shelley, right?"

My heart started to pound.

"I thought you knew."

"Shelley lived next door? You mean I grew up right next door?"

There was silence on the other end.

My head couldn't get around it. "But I don't…" I said "Why did you choose her?"

"Oh. Well, she was your babysitter. She didn't tell you?"

I was so confused. "Shelley babysat me?"

"I thought she would've told you. When your mother went to prison…Well, Shelley was already looking after you. And she wanted to adopt you. We thought it would be less disruptive if you stayed with someone you were used to."

"Oh. I…um…" My brain wasn't working.

"She really wanted you. I thought it was a good fit. We even gave her the piano so you could learn to play."

So that's where it came from. I learned to play on my mother's piano!

"Did things work out okay with her?"

"I…um…"

"Sounds to me like you better have a talk with her."

After hanging up, I ran to my night table. I pulled out the photo of my mother and me on the stoop of the house. It had looked familiar. Now I knew why. It was just like the stoop at Shelley's because it was next door. The houses were the same style. My family lived next door to Shelley. And she never said.

I punched in Shelley's cell on speed dial. She sometimes worked late on Fridays. But it was nearly seven.

"Hello?"

"Where are you?" I said.

"I just got home…"

"I need to talk to you." I hung up and grabbed my purse.

* * *

I walked down Maple Glen Avenue, seeing it for the first time. I grew up on this street, but now it looked strange and unfamiliar. I could've been dreaming. Only the dream was a nightmare.

I stopped in front of 140, the house next door. It looked just like Shelley's. Three wooden stairs leading up to a porch. That day in the old photo, we sat on the top step, my mother and me. I felt like I'd been sleep-walking my whole life. This was my house. Where I lived with my real parents. Where my father had come home one night and…

It had been there this whole time, waiting for me. Someone else lived there now. This was the house where I was happy with my mom and dad.

I walked up the stairs to Shelley's. My stomach twisted. Nothing had changed but me. My whole life was a lie.

I opened the door and walked in. Shelley stood there, a funny look on her face, like she didn't know what to say. I'd dyed her hair mauve-red for the fall, but it was straggly now, like she hadn't washed it in days. She kept it long, which usually made her look younger. But now she looked tired. Tired and old.

"Why didn't you tell me about next door?"

She stiffened. "Nothing to tell."

"I lived there with my parents! My *real* parents!"

She flinched.

I wanted to hurt her.

"I was trying to protect you," she said.

"Why didn't you tell me you babysat me?"

She blinked, like she had something in her eye.

"You knew my mother! What was she like?"

"I'm your mother."

She obviously wasn't going to be reasonable. "What was Carol Allan like?"

She licked her lips, not eager to go on. "She didn't get it. How lucky she was. She had everything. Freddy. You. She was always going out. Teaching piano. I was the one who looked after you. I'm your mother."

"You hated her, didn't you?"

"You shouldn't speak ill of the dead."

"Did you see her do it?" I don't know what made me ask that. Gave me shivers.

She looked at me, surprised. Her mouth opened, but nothing came out.

"Tell me!" I said.

"The truth is ugly. You don't want it."

"You were right here!" I cried. I was losing control, but I had to know. "You saw everything!"

Her eyes flashed. "What did that bitch tell you?"

We seemed to be in two different conversations. "Who?"

"That junkie Diane. Don't believe anything she said."

"You knew her?"

She blinked at me. I had caught her in something. I just didn't know what.

"I don't know her," she said. "She called once. Introduced herself."

Then I remembered something. I opened my purse and pulled out Diane's cell. I'd forgotten to ditch it. I scrolled through her last phone calls. There it was. Diane *had* called Shelley. At least four times. And Shelley had called Diane. The day she died.

"How'd you know she was a junkie?"

She didn't look me in the eye. "You told me she OD'd."

"I never said! You know she OD'd because you were there."

"Better leave things alone, Amanda."

"Did you help her OD? Were you there?"

Something changed in her eyes. I had a sense she was giving up.

"Did you kill her?"

Shelley hung her head. She swallowed. "Once a user, always a user," she said. "Didn't take much."

My heart fell. I wanted her to deny it.

"She was no good, Amanda. She was trying to shake me down. Said she'd go to the cops and tell her lies if I didn't give her money."

"I feel sick," I said. I went into the kitchen in case I had to throw up. She followed me.

"What could she tell the cops?" I said, standing near the sink.

"Ancient history. Forget it."

"Tell me or I'm leaving." I looked at her. She knew I meant for good.

She stared at me, her eyes big and round. "It was…about your father and me…"

I swallowed and stared at her. Yeah, Shelley had been hot twenty years ago, but I hadn't expected this. "You…slept with my father?"

"It wasn't like that…" She took a breath. "One day Freddy came home early. I was there alone with you. He was something, your dad. He had a way about him—I can't explain. We…we hit it off. I was a knock-out in those days. Carol wasn't enough for him."

I closed my eyes. I didn't want to hear.

She rubbed her eyes. "But then, after a while, I wasn't enough for him either. He was always looking for something… new. I was so nuts about him. I thought we'd get married."

She licked her lips. "One day out of the blue he said he didn't want to see me anymore."

"You were the neighbor who told the cops they fought all the time."

"Men are such stupid romantics. He said he still loved her. He didn't even look at me when I talked to him."

So he was leaving all those other women behind for my mother. We would've been a family again.

I prayed I was wrong. "What happened?"

She covered her eyes with her hand. "I was hurting so much. It made me crazy. He threw me away. Like I was nothing."

"It was *you*…"

"No! You don't understand. I loved him. I never meant to…"

She leaned forward and started to whisper, like someone else could hear. "I'm not a bad person. I was so desperate…That night, it was so cold. I waited outside for him with my winter jacket on. Honestly, I just wanted to scare him. I told him I was going to kill Carol. So I brought the knife."

I gasped and she looked at me as if she saw something different in me. My mother?

"Oh no, I never would've hurt her, I'd never…"

"You were wearing gloves! That's why there were no fingerprints."

She turned away and stared into space. "When he thought I was going after

Carol—he just went wild! He tried to grab the knife and we struggled and…I just… I didn't mean…" She leaned back, pale.

I closed my eyes and covered my mouth with my hands. It was some kind of instinct to keep the scream from coming out and breaking me apart. The room got very close and I could hardly breathe. The old Shelley would've put her arm around my shoulder to comfort me. I opened my eyes to see if I still recognized her. She was leaning against the counter, staring at the steak knives that stuck out of the wooden stand. She was close enough to reach one.

"You going to kill me too?"

She put her hand up to her forehead. "What?"

"All these years you pretended to love me."

Tears filled her eyes. "No, baby. I always loved you. You were the best thing that ever happened to me. You were his. I had part of him with me. I'm not a strong person. I didn't have the guts to confess and go to jail. I felt terrible about Carol. But then, like a miracle—you needed me. No one ever needed me."

I hated her. She stole my life. She was a psycho. She was a slut. She was... the only mother I remembered. I couldn't think.

"I have to call the cops," I said quietly.

She nodded.

"I'll give you a head start."

She looked down at the floor. "Where am I going to go? You're all I've got."

I still had Diane's cell in my hand. I sat down at the table, shaking. I *hated* Shelley. But I had this picture of us in the kitchen when I was little and she made me breakfast. She knew how I liked my eggs. And after school she'd wait for me at home, so happy to see me. Sometimes when I was really miserable she'd hold me…

Through my tears, I punched in Randall Webb's number. She'd need a lawyer.

CHAPTER TWELVE

Shelley surrendered to the police accompanied by Randall Webb. He told me the police were shocked to receive a new confession in a case that had been solved twenty years earlier. They had no evidence to link her to Freddy's murder and, in view of the confession, recommended the court be lenient. But not for Diane's death. Shelley had left her fingerprints in the flat. They locked her up and denied bail.

I didn't really want to see her again. But I wasn't sure I could keep away. She still *felt* like my mother, in spite of everything. How could that be?

She called me from jail to say Happy Birthday. We pretended like nothing was wrong. It was weird talking to her. But she was one of the only people who knew, or cared, that it was my birthday.

Over the next month, I tried to take my mind off everything with music. After my day at the salon, I'd come home at night and write edgy songs about love and hate, and how hard it was to tell them apart.

Brooke called a few times to check on me. I felt a connection. Maybe she did too. Stu had taken off to some casino or other to do his thing.

Brooke said she wanted to hear my songs. I was in kind of a funk, so she had to ask a few times. But one day I kicked myself and said to the mirror: *This is what you wanted. Get your butt out there.* Besides, it was a chance to see my brother.

So on one of my days off, I went to the club, lugging my Gibson. I'd never played my music for anyone else. I sat on the low stage—scared and hyper. I bent over my guitar. Didn't want to see Brooke's and Lexy's eyes on me. Afraid of what they'd see.

They loved it. Brooke smiled and Lexy clapped like crazy after each number. I did three.

"That's some serious music!" Brooke said. "We have a winter show for new talent. Seven or eight musicians. Each gets to do two songs. You interested?"

Was I interested! "That would be awesome!"

"I'll put your name down."

While Brooke headed for the door, Lexy came toward me. "Those songs are amazing," he said, a big grin on his face. "Wanna jam some time? Maybe we could do a song together."

"Wicked!" I felt stupidly happy.

Brooke stood near the door, watching. Nervous, I thought.

"Wanna get some coffee?" he said.

"Sure." I added, "Then I have to meet my boyfriend."

His face fell. But Brooke's brightened up. She was probably worried about two things—one, Lexy would fall for me, his half sister. Or two, I would spill the beans about his father. She didn't have to worry. It was her business what she told her kid. I wasn't going to piss her off—she was going to give me my big break. Besides, I liked her. And my imaginary boyfriend could stick around in case Lexy got romantic. He was a good musician and I was looking forward to jamming with him. Maybe we'd form a new band. I could be a big sister to him.

SYLVIA MAULTASH WARSH is the author of the Dr. Rebecca Temple mystery series set in 1979 Toronto. The first book, *To Die in Spring,* was nominated for an Arthur Ellis Award in 2001; the second, *Find Me Again,* won an Edgar Award in 2004; the third, *Season of Iron,* was shortlisted for a ReLit Award in 2007. Sylvia lives in Toronto with her family.